Gadget Hero

by Lisa Thompson
illustrated by Lisa Thompson
and
Matthew Stapleton

PICTURE WINDOW BOOKS
Minneapolis, Minnesota

Editor: Jacqueline A. Wolfe
Managing Editor: Catherine Neitge
Story Consultant: Terry Flaherty
Page Production: Melissa Kes
Creative Director: Keith Griffin
Editorial Director: Carol Jones

First American edition published in 2006 by
Picture Window Books
5115 Excelsior Boulevard
Suite 232
Minneapolis, MN 55416
1-877-845-8392
www.picturewindowbooks.com

First published in Australia in 2004 by
Blake Publishing Pty Ltd
ABN 50 074 266 023
108 Main Rd
Clayton South VIC 3168

© Blake Publishing Pty Ltd Australia 2004

Printed in the United States of America.

Library of Congress Cataloging-in-Publication Data
Thompson, Lisa, 1969-
The gadget hero / by Lisa Thompson ; illustrated by Lisa Thompson and Matthew Stapleton.—
1st American ed.
p. cm. — (Read-it! chapter books) (Wonder wits)
Summary: When Luke and Sophie are school-newspaper reporters at a Gadget Fair, they notice
small signs in strange spots around the building saying "Thanks Hero," and they set out to find
out who is behind the signs.
ISBN 1-4048-1349-7 (hardcover)
1. Hero, of Alexandria—Juvenile fiction. [1. Hero, of Alexandria—Fiction. 2. Inventors—
Fiction.] I. Stapleton, Matthew, ill. II. Title. III. Series.
PZ7.T371634Gad 2005
[Fic]—dc22
2005009825

Table of Contents

"Hey, Soph, check this out," Luke said. He showed his best friend, Sophie, a small tool shaped like a pen. "The inventor says this tiny thing can do five hundred different tasks—from zapping cockroaches to cutting through tin. It's called the Amaze-All. Maybe this is what we're after."

Latest wonder gadget, the Amaze-All,

Sophie shook her head. "It's not the kind of amazing we're after."

Luke and Sophie were at the Gadget Fair looking for a story for the school paper. Sophie didn't want to write about the latest wonder gadget. She wanted to find something special. They had looked at lots of booths but hadn't found the right thing.

can do 500 different tasks!!!!

"Let's check the displays on the next level,"
Sophie said.

"I need to get a drink first," said Luke, spotting a
vending machine on the other side of the hall.

Sophie and Luke noticed a lady near the machine
looking through her purse. She pulled out a sign and
stuck it next to the money slot on the vending machine.

Signs saying THANKS HERO were

The sign read THANKS HERO.

Luke and Sophie had noticed these signs in
other parts of the building. They'd seen them on
the automatic doors at the entrance, and the
model jet plane in the lobby.

They walked over to the vending machine. The
woman stood there, admiring her sign. Sophie
couldn't contain her curiosity and asked, "Excuse
me. What are these signs for?"

popping up all over the place.

The woman looked pleased by Sophie's question. "They're to get people thinking about where these ideas came from," she explained. "Many people think we only began inventing machines recently. But many of the machines we use started out 2,000 years ago. The ancient Greek inventor Hero of Alexandria made gadgets that have given us good ideas today." She nodded at the sign.

Many people think we only began inventing

"Are you an inventor?" asked Luke.

"Not really." The woman smiled. "My name is Angela Richards. I'm president of the Hero Appreciation Society. We want to make people realize that Hero was a great inventor. Many of the things they use each day are based on his ideas. He really was ahead of his time." She looks at the crowd. "If only everyone knew!"

gadgets and machines recently.

Luke put his money into the machine and got his drink.

"Hero invented the first coin-operated machine," said Miss Richards proudly, as if she had done it herself.

"Two thousand years ago?" Luke asked.

Miss Richards nodded. "Of course, it wasn't an electric one like this, but the idea for the machine was the same."

She continued, "Hero also made automatic doors, a steam-powered engine, talking statues, mechanical birds, robots, a wind organ, and many other great creations."

"Wow!" said Luke. He looked at Sophie to see what she thought.

Sophie was beaming. "I think we might have found our story. Miss Richards, would you mind telling us more about Hero so we can write about him in our school paper?"

was invented 2,000 years ago.

"I'd love to spread the word about Hero!" said
Miss Richards. "We should start by looking at
perhaps his most famous invention—the aeolipile.
Aeolipile means 'wind ball.' It's the basis of a jet
engine. There's one on the fifth floor."

Miss Richards looked through her bag and pulled
out more THANKS HERO signs. She handed one
to Sophie.

"I'd love to spread the

"Could you stick one of these on the elevator doors as you go up?" Miss Richards asked. "I don't think the automatic doors of today are half as impressive as Hero's. Anyway, I have a few more signs to put up, and then I'll be finished. See you soon!" she said, before disappearing with her bag of signs.

word about Hero!"

The Hero Appreciation Society met in a large room on the fifth floor. One wall was covered with drawings of Hero's inventions. Luke and Sophie were surprised by how many inventions there were. There were pictures of toys, fountains, surveying instruments, and machinery. There were even math formulas!

Hero's inventions range from simple and

"That must be the wind ball," said Luke, pointing to a strange device at one end of the room.

A large, sealed cauldron of water was built over a gas burner. Two pipes led from the cauldron to a hollow ball. On opposite sides of the ball were two small, L-shaped tubes. Sophie touched the ball and saw that it could spin.

The hotter the water, the faster the ball spins!

1. Water heats up and makes the steam.

"I see you found it!" said Miss Richards, hurrying into the room. "It doesn't look like much at first because it is so simple. That's what is fantastic about it. Let me start it up for you. We have it working at all our meetings." Miss Richards pushed a lever on the machine. "Of course, Hero didn't have a gas burner to heat the water, but it's easier for us than building a fire with wood."

The wind ball is the basis

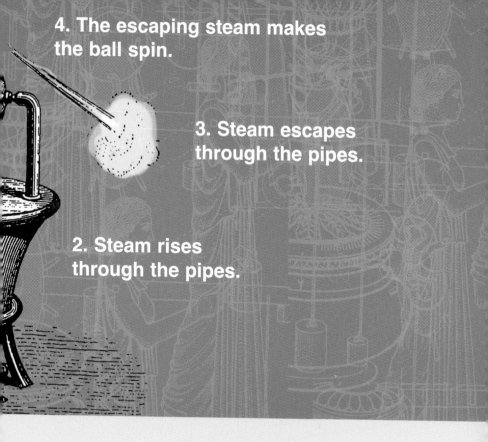

4. The escaping steam makes the ball spin.

3. Steam escapes through the pipes.

2. Steam rises through the pipes.

She smiled. "Otherwise, it works just as Hero intended."

When the water heated up, steam traveled through the two pipes into the ball. The steam escaped through the two L-shaped tubes, making the ball spin. As the water got hotter and more steam was produced, the ball spun even faster.

of today's jet engine.

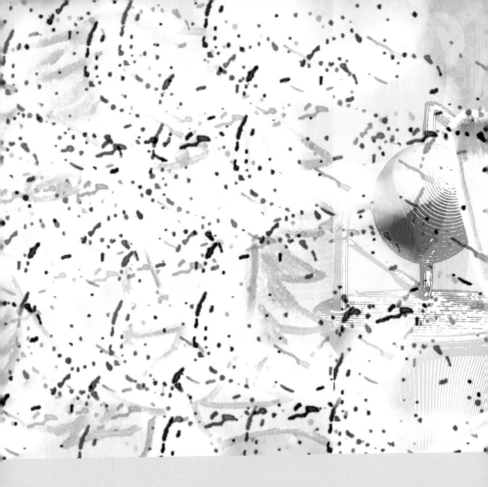

"This was the first steam-powered engine!" Miss Richards said. "It's the same idea used in jet engines and spinning garden sprinklers. It's such a simple idea for creating power!" She turned down the fire.

It's the same principle used in steam and jet

"Who would have believed it would be at least another 1,500 years before the first steam engine was actually built?" Miss Richards asked.

"Why didn't Hero build one himself?" asked Luke. "Didn't he know what to use his invention for?"

"The ancient world didn't really need steam
engines because slaves did all the work. Since
there was no real need, no one took the trouble to
develop it. At that time, the wind ball was an
invention without a job! Hero's work was forgotten
about for centuries," sighed Miss Richards.

Hero's wind ball was an

"It was an idea before its time," said Sophie, quickly writing notes.

"Exactly!" agreed Miss Richards. "But he also invented things that caused great wonder in his own time. He loved designing things that baffled people. I'll show you some."

idea way ahead of its time!

Chapter 3
Fire, Weights, Water, and Steam

Miss Richards led them back to the wall. She pointed to drawings of an old slot machine, a tiny theater with statues of people inside, and automatic doors.

"Hero was great at making machines that could run on their own after being set in motion," she told them.

Many of Hero's inventions could operate

"Hero's machines used weights, fire, water, and steam. Some were quite simple, like this slot machine used in the temples," Miss Richards explained.

"How did it work?" asked Luke.

"Like many of Hero's gadgets, it used a simple balance system," said Miss Richards.

on their own after being set in motion.

"The idea was to put a coin in the slot to get holy water. The coin fell into a pan that hung from one end of a carefully balanced beam. The weight of the coin made one end of the beam go down and the other end rise," Miss Richards said.

Hero's holy water dispenser was

"The raised end opened a valve that let water flow out. When the coin fell off the pan, the beam became level again. Then the valve would close, and the flow of water would stop," said Miss Richards.

"That's so simple!" said Sophie, but she could see Miss Richards had even more great things to share.

the world's first vending machine.

Miss Richards pointed to the drawing of a temple door. "With these designs for the automatic door, Hero became a high-tech inventor of the ancient world. He even figured out how to make a trumpet blow when the door opened!"

"Was that the first automatic doorbell?" joked Sophie.

"Or the first burglar alarm," added Luke.

The inventions relied on fire, weights,

"Perhaps it was both," smiled Miss Richards. "Hero designed his doors to work by a system of fire, air, water, weights, and pulleys." She pointed to different parts of the drawing as she explained. "The priest lit a fire on the altar. Underneath the altar was a container of water."

water, and pulleys to work.

Mrs. Richards continued, "The air in the container was heated by the fire. The hot air pushed the water through a pipe into a bucket. When the bucket got heavy enough, it pulled on chains and the doors opened. Of course, all that people saw was a fire being lit and a little while later the doors opening, as if by magic!"

Hero's inventions amazed all who saw them.

Luke scanned the wall. "What about this plan for a tiny theater?"

Miss Richards' eyes lit up. "It's wonderful! Hero invented this to put on a real show. Doors opened and closed, tiny altars lit up, and little figures moved around and made noises," she exclaimed.

Some thought they worked by magic.

"The whole thing was operated by gravity and used weights, ropes, wheels, and bits of grain or sand that fell through devices like egg timers," said Miss Richards.

"Where did Hero come up with so many ideas? And where did he test them out?" asked Luke.

Hero lived in Alexandria, The City

"Hero lived in a place called Alexandria. During his time, it was a city of ideas." Miss Richards opened a long, thin drawer in a filing cabinet. "I'll show you artists' drawings of ancient Alexandria so you can see what the city looked like," she said.

"Two thousand years ago," explained Miss Richards, pointing to an old map, "Alexandria was a huge city on the coast of Egypt. Lots of people traveled there for trade. It was also a magnet for scientists, philosophers, and great inventors."

Alexandria was a bustling Greek

She continued, "It is recorded that Alexandria had a library and a museum. The museum held classes in many subjects. It was a place where people with lots of different interests could come together to share ideas."

"Was Hero a member of the museum?" asked Sophie.

"Yes. Hero wasn't just an inventor. He also taught math and science."

"So homework existed even in the first century!" laughed Luke.

"Did teaching math and science give Hero ideas for inventions?" asked Sophie.

Many great thinkers flocked

"I'm sure it helped. Many other experts in different fields surrounded Hero. He could share his ideas with them, and they could help to figure out problems," said Miss Richards. "But the museum wasn't the only place he shared his ideas. He also wrote books filled with ideas for other inventions that he thought might work, and tips on how to be a great inventor."

to Alexandria to share ideas.

make models

record

experiment

look

compare and share ideas

Miss Richards continued, "Hero wrote that inventors needed to look at things from different ways. They needed to experiment, record, make models, discuss theories, compare and share ideas, and think 'what if.' Sometimes Hero built models like the wind ball simply because the idea seemed interesting. Hero had the inventor's gift of always being curious."

"What happened to the library?" asked Luke. "Where are all the books?"

The library and museum in Alexandria held the

"The library and the museum were destroyed during war. Most of Hero's notes and records of his inventions were lost for over one thousand five hundred years," said Miss Richards.

"Yet the ideas survived, and we use them today," added Sophie.

"Imagine if they had never been lost!" said Luke.

"Yes," said Miss Richards, shaking her head. "Just imagine what other things might have been invented by now."

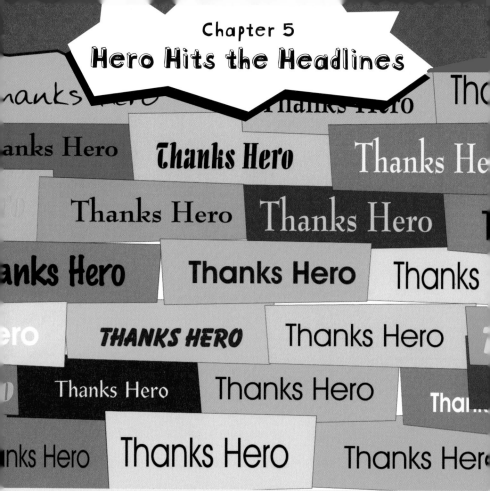

In the days leading up to the next issue of the school paper, signs saying THANKS HERO appeared around the school. They were found on automatic doors, drinking fountains, and vending machines. THANKS HERO Post-it-notes were even found in library books about steam trains and jet engines.

THANKS HERO Thanks Hero Thanks He

Hero Thanks Hero Thanks Hero

Thanks Hero Thanks Hero Thanks

ks Hero Thanks Hero THANKS HE

Thanks Hero Thanks Hero Tha

KS HERO Thanks Hero Thanks H
ks Hero

No one in the school, except for Luke, Sophie, and the paper's editor, had any idea what the signs meant. Everyone wondered who Hero was and tried to guess where the next sign might appear.

Adding to the mystery was the aeolipile on display in the school library. Miss Richards and the Hero Appreciation Society had loaned their replica for the display.

Thanks Hero Thanks Hero

The librarian ran a competition. She asked students to guess the aeolipile's purpose. No one guessed it was the first steam-powered engine.

Finally the day came when the story was revealed. All copies of the paper were snapped up as people rushed to find out who Hero was, and what the strange thing in the library did.

What is it???? Any guesses???? It's the

Miss Richards was thrilled when Luke and Sophie gave her a copy of the paper and she saw the headline:

HERO REVEALED!
MEET THE INVENTOR WHOSE IDEAS
ARE EVERYWHERE.

"This article is great!" she cried. "Everyone who reads this will know that Hero was a great inventor and that many of the things we use today are a result of his ideas!"

world's first steam-powered engine!

"As president of the Hero Appreciation Society, I am making you both members of our club," announced Miss Richards. "You can share ideas with us and experiment with other inventors, just as Hero did. You might even invent things that shape the future and will be used in thousands of years—just like Hero!"

Congratulations! You are now official life

"I'd like that!" said Sophie, smiling. "What about you, Luke?"

"Yeah, I'm sure I can come up with an invention," he laughed. "And I think a Luke Appreciation Society sounds very exciting!"

Vending Machine Madness

When Hero invented his holy water dispensing machine, he had no idea he had invented a machine that would become one of the most convenient and popular ways of selling products in the future—the vending machine. Among other things, you can actually find live worms, fresh food, and cell phones in vending machines.

underwear, pajamas, dried

squid, fresh steaks, tickets,

herbal remedies, pearl

necklaces, books, soft drinks,

tea, coffee, bags of rice,

batteries, jeans, eggs,

notebooks, bread, newspapers,

videotapes, live shrimp,

frogs, fresh fish, worms, suckers, fortune cookies, fortune-telling cards, temporary tattoos, beef jerky, comic books, business cards, stuffed animals, watches, cameras, envelopes, stamps, flower arrangements, badges, shavers, calculators, coffee, eans, panty hose, poetry, books, sandwiches, chips, ink, gas, hot noodles, vegetables, tennis balls, hamburgers, dog tags, pizza, umbrellas, soap, toothbrushes, shower caps, socks, playing cards, chess and checker sets, sewing kits, popcorn, perfume, magazines, sweat bands, maps, shaving cream,

... The list goes on ...

herbal eye pillows, night crawlers, car rentals, cell phones, coupons, sunscreen, raincoats, insurance, postcards, shopping cards, permits, orange juice, corn, fish food, duck food, tuna fish, beetles, snow globes, rocks, rulers, pens, pencils ...

what have YOU seen?

Read all about Luke and Sophie's unusual adventures in these great books!

1. Artrageous
2. Wonder Worlds
3. Wild Ideas
4. Look Out!
5. What's Next?
6. Game Plan
7. Gadget Hero
8. Bony Puzzle